MILES OMEGA

BloodMoon Novella

Mercy Ashes

Mercy Ashes

To Shirley,
a Pre christmas
treat ♡.

Mercy
Ashes
♡

CONTENTS

TRIGGER WARNINGS

This Novella is based around
Miles's Heat.

Miles's Harem is complete with four males,
so expect Male on Male action.

Miles is with all envolved.
Brayden is only with Miles.
Bramley and Matteo are with each other and Miles.

There are a mix of these in the scenes.

If you feel I have missed anything in my trigger
warning please let me know.

JUST SO YOU KNOW :)

This Novella takes part at the
end of Chapter eight.

A Phoenix Will Rise,
Book Two
The BloodMoon Trilogy

It is recommended that you read book one and
two of the BloodMoon series first.

Thank you.
X

THE TRIPLEMOON FAMILY TREE

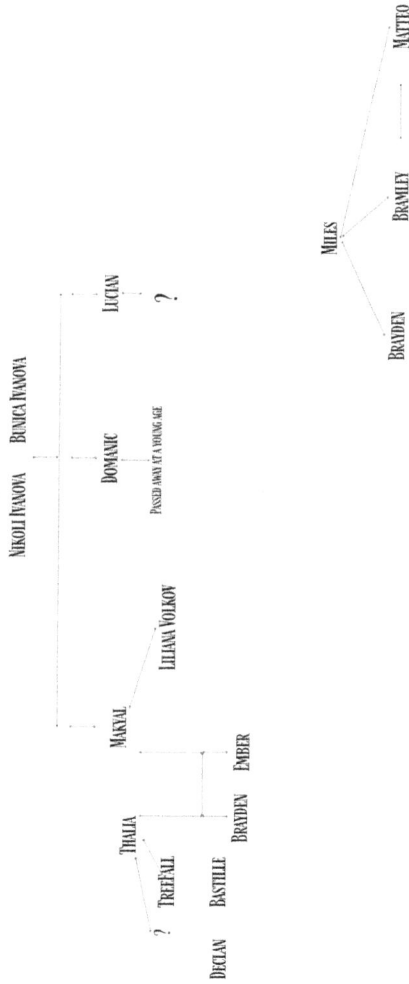

Nikoli Ivanova — Bunica Ivanova

Domanic
Passed away at a young age

Lucian
?

Maykal — Liliana Volkow

Thalia
?

TreeFall

Bastille

Declan

Braden

Ember

Miles

Braden

Bramley — Matteo

MILES

The two weeks moved slowly to Mateos arrival, we texted, and video called all the time even when he's sitting reading in his office and he was just there it has helped with the heat symptoms, Kodi, Ember and Bray went off to help him move, he can drive but until his promotion, he couldn't afford a car.

Em has messaged Pops to find one for him, and he has a Jeep Cherokee that needs a tune; it's a really pretty silver colour. Pops tried to give it as a gift, but Ember pointed out that he wouldn't accept it. So, Pops said he could pay a bit each payday instead of a lump sum, but at least then he could get to and from work without hassle.

I kept trying to do more in his room and office but like Em pointed out we didn't know what he was bringing with him but she did tell me his office at work was a little impersonal so I have been sorting some photos and things to be taken in, including some empty ones so we can add new photos. Em found one of the two of them in college. The guy next to them was asleep in the lecture with a straw from his drink up his nose, and they were pulling funny faces. Em knocked him up some Canvases to add some colour.

"Babe, they just got to the gate. Stay here while we get everything in, okay?" Bram kisses my temple and shuts my door as he heads down to help. I finish getting my nest all set up and clean my already clean bathroom. I hear a roar and then the woosh of wings, but I don't feel any panic in the air, so I continue to potter around my room, twisting a couple of my blankets as they aren't quite right.

BRAM

I leave Miles's room, between us and Ember we agreed to get Matt in before we risk setting off Miles's full heat, I reach the bottom of the step, just as they are getting out of the car, I feel my eyes change to those of my blood dragon.

"MINE!!!!" Ember spins eyes wide.

"Go fly it off Bram before you hurt Matt or Miles, bring us something tasty home," she knew I was on tender hooks of my control; I nod and superman jump shifting midair, wonder what Mateo likes to eat, I circle our woods looking for the perfect offering to welcome our new mate. I spot some deer and head towards them. I scoop up a stag and a few others, then drop them behind the kitchen, the animals dying as they thump to the floor, screams ring out, and my dragon chuffs when we spot that stupid blonde succubus that was causing problems for our sister.

EMBER

I watch Bram fly off as Bray appears at my shoulder.

"Okay?" he seems unsure, watching Bram's retreat.

"Yeah, problem with Dragon hybrids, his Vampire side heightens his Dragon's need to Claim and poses his ultimate treasure, he just needs to ease the blood lust before being near them, it's why I told him to bring home something tasty, animal instinct is to provide for his mate, best warm Alma." He just grunts, and we start to take stuff in. It doesn't take long, and we soon hear a scream, then a thud.

"Sounds like Bram bought a few home," I open Miles's door,

"Bram reacted to Matt's scent, and he went hunting. He might be a little rougher and more demanding, but he won't hurt you." I don't enter Miles's room, which has turned into a nest since I left a few hours ago. I feel a powerful pulse from Miles as Bray and Matt appear next to me; the scent coming from Miles makes me feel sick, which is a defence to non-mates. Bram storms past me, dripping blood everywhere. He pulls Matt into a Kiss, and if these guys weren't practically my brothers, it would be hot. I can see the effect the view is having on Miles,

"MINE!" Bram growls before throwing Miles over his shoulder.

"But first I need to please our needy omega", he stomps to the bathroom, spanking a giggling, swooning Miles on the butt as he goes – well, ok then, action stations.

**ME: Can you send Miles
heat supplies up, please. x**

RIVER: Incoming. x

Shadows appear on and next to the desk and cases of water, sports drinks, and snacky foods appear.

"Matt, go grab some clothes and whatever if you're staying. Bray, you may want to do the same. Only Bray can text Me for extra supplies as I'm female and his sister, I will be the only non-threat for the next week, it was Miles's idea or his alter will take it as you rejecting him," I say looking at Matt, as Miles moans drift from the bathroom and Matt and Bray walk back in I head off.
"Have fun, guys, see you in a week."

MILES

"Bram reacted to Matt's scent, and he went hunting. He might be a little rougher and more demanding, but he won't hurt you." Ember says before I catch Mateos' scent and drop to my knees with a whimper.

"You're okay, kitten." Bray appears at my side, stroking my back,

"Hurts," I whimper out before anyone can speak. Bram stomps in dripping blood over my pretty nest,

"MINE," he rumbles, taking Mateo's mouth in a deep, claiming kiss. I notice Mateo's knees are weakening,

"Mine." Bram again growls against his lips as he stops the kiss, spinning on his heel, he throws me over his shoulder,

"But first, I need to please our omega." He slaps my ass as he stomps into the bathroom and flips on the shower. I'm on my feet, mine and his clothes are torn from our bodies, and within seconds of us being naked, I'm lifted into his arms, my legs wrapped around his waist, and my back pressed to the cold tile.

He rinses off the blood, he's so focused on cleaning me, and all I can think about is licking the bead of precum I can see on the tip of his thick cock.

"Mine, My mate, My perfect omega, My gorgeous kitty," he says between kisses. I grind my hips against him, giving us both friction, his huge hands holding my ass, our hardness rubbing against each other with each roll of my hips,

"Please," I whimper to my Dragon, my precum leaking against his chiselled abs. I don't fully know what I want, but he seems to, gripping my ass tighter, he pushes me up 'thank the goddess for high ceilings' he laps at my balls before sliding my painfully hard cock into his hot mouth,

"Yes," I gasp as a kitten purr starts in my chest, he moves his grip on me, and then I feel a thick finger start circling my puckered hole,

"Oh, Bram, please, I need you, my fierce Dragon." I feel his chuckle around my length, I can also feel his fangs lengthen on either side, adding to the sensations,

"Is my kitty slick for my fingers, I want your cream on my tongue before you get my cock in this tight hole," his voice is just a rumble and I can feel my body tremble with anticipation, his thick finger presses into where I need it, my cock back in his mouth before I can form words,

"Bram, I need more," I whimper as the shower is turned off, my eyes fly open to see my Wolf dressed only in boxers.

"Then cum down his throat and get on the bed so he can fill that pretty ass with his cock while I fill my kitten's mouth with mine," he turns, letting his boxers fall to the floor, he kneels up on the bed waiting for me.

I catch sight of Mateo stroking his trouser-covered cock at the sight of Bram and me, yeah, I'm done, sending hot spurts of cream into my Dragon's mouth, the rumble of Bram's happiness setting me off again prolonging my pleasure.

BRAYDEN

I head to the room and kneel on the bed, resting my ass on my heels as I wait for my mate. I can smell his heat, and I want to lock myself away just me and him, but he has two other mates.

I'm not jealous of them, but I do enjoy being the only one pleasing my mate, knowing every gasp and moan I caused.

I've talked a lot to my sister's mates about the sharing thing. Ren is the easiest, and he's admitted he must remind himself not to be selfish a lot. Pine confirmed that once she is pregnant with his pups, he won't feel it as much, but I don't think Miles is ready for babies yet, even though the thought of my twin's babies growing up alongside mine fills my heart, knowing they get what we missed out on.

Before the hate towards our incubator starts to take a form, Bram walks out of the Bathroom carrying my Kitten.

If I didn't know I bought Miles pleasure, I would be thinking of ways of removing that monster from between Bram's legs. I inwardly chuckle at the thought of Miles walking stiffly after taking all of us.

Bram places Miles on the edge of the bed, and my perfect kitten crawls towards me. I already have my cock in hand stroking it, he licks the tip before going on his knees and kissing me deeply, his purr making me harder.

He leaves my mouth kissing along my jaw, down my neck, and over my chest, and the brat nips at my nipples as he passes them. He nibbles at my abs, his hard cock leaving a trail as it brushes against me. 'Fun fact when male Omegas are in heat their cock is permanently hard, and their ass leaks slick like a female's pussy,' so no need for lube or waiting for him to get hard again.

His mouth sucks along my shaft, leaving little love bites until he reaches my tip, where he laps at my slit.

I stroke his hair, loving the pleasure on his face at his actions.

I glance at Bram as Miles slides my cock down his throat. Kitten has no gag reflex, so he takes all of me, swallowing around my length. Bram is tongue deep in Matt's mouth, with his hand around his impressive dick,

"Bring him here, Bram, let Miles drink his cream down, I've changed my mind, my Cum is going in our Brats' needy ass, not down his throat." I feel Miles's whimper around my cock, smirking down at him,

"Mmm, do you like the sound of that? our omega being the first to taste this thick cock?" Bram growls against Matt's ear and his eyes glow red as he manoeuvres himself into the nest, he then grabs Miles's hips and with a swat to his perk ass,

"Swallow Mateos cock like a good omega while I sink into this dripping hole," I hear Matt whimper and whisper a

"Please" as Miles looks at me asking with his eyes if he's allowed before taking Matt into his mouth, his eyes rolling to the back of his head as Bram sinks into him, Bram leans forward and pulls Matt back into a kiss before taking Miles hard and fast, Brams face is euphoric, I remember the first time I sank balls deep into Miles, I still never want to leave

"He likes being spanked, Dragon, his ass tightens like a vice," I husk stroking my cock at the view I have, Bram smirks and his tail appears swatting Matt's ass as he uses his hand to spank Miles, the following deep chuckle confirms Matt likes it too.

I twist around and slide below Miles, taking his pretty cock in my mouth, before taking it back out,

"You going to come, kitten, so your dragon can fill that tight hole of yours?" It doesn't take long before all three of them are moaning out their release. I don't unless it's inside my mate, I won't cum.

MILES

I cum in Brayden's mouth as Mateo fills mine, Bramley's cock is pulsing inside me.

"Good little kitty, suck down my cream into this slick little hole," he rumbles before flopping onto the bed next to Mateo. I crawl straight onto Bray's lap, he didn't cum, and that's not okay with me.

Grabbing his cock and lining it up to my ass, I sink onto him, he's smaller than Bram, but he has a slight curve, so it hits where I need him,

"Fuck kitten, feels so good, ride me, baby, take everything you need," my cock rubs against his abs as I lean forward for a kiss, he cups my ass helping me bounce, I love Bray have for a long time, and I know he likes one on one time but I need more cocks inside me, I need to have cum dripping from my flesh.

"More, please. so full but need more," I pant against his lips. Bray moves one hand from my ass to my cock, stroking me in time with my thrusts, and his other hand moves to my nape.

"CUM", he growls before sinking his teeth into my shoulder.

"Yes fuck Yes, I'm yours, fuck yes, Yes, YEs, YES" I chant as he fills my ass with his cum, once he lets go of my shoulder I move quickly off him so I can sink my teeth into his abs, before pumping my cock furiously so my cum covers my bite mark, he grabs my jaw, kissing me hard before snarling at me.

"Lick your cream up and seal that mark, kitten." And I do I greedily lap all my cum from his body, taking care to seal the mark. I feel a hand run down my spine, and I glance over my shoulder.

"Do you need more, pretty mate?" Mateo asks as he cups my hips.

"Goddess, yes, please." I wiggle my ass at him before turning back, and continuing to clean Bray's already half-hard cock, I love that shifters get hard so quickly; I feel for poor humans who have to wait.

MATEO

At Miles's Plea, I wait for Bray's nod that he needs a break before I roll Miles onto his back. Positioning myself between his legs, I kiss him like he's the air I breathe, but my omega is still needy, and he starts to whimper. Still kissing him, I move so I can slide my eager cock into his slick, puckered hole,

"Fuck *my heart.*" I don't pound into him like Bram did. I make love to him, slow and so fucking deep, I have no idea how I don't cum in seconds,

"Mark me *my heart,*" he doesn't hesitate to sink his teeth into my collarbone, I stroke my thumb over my Pinky ring, saying the spell I need to seal my soul to his, somewhere an extra mark will appear on him as my claim.

His rough tongue laps at his bite, and his hips start to can't with mine, my abs are not as defined as Bray's or chiselled at Bram's, but with his perfect cock rubbing against me, I feel like an Adonis.

"I love you," he breathes against my neck as we come together,

"I love you too, *my heart,*" I murmur as I hold him, both of us falling asleep.

I wake to the feel of a warm cloth running over my abs,

"It's just me, little mage, just freshening you up before our little omega becomes demanding again," he presses a kiss to my lips, and in my half-asleep mind, it makes sense. I rub my ring and think the spell to seal us together.

"Cheeky little mage," I'm spun and on top of Bram, his cock pressed between my lips

"Now my turn to mark you," he takes my cock in his mouth, and I feel his hand shift on my ass.

MILES

I wake to the sounds of moans and the feel of Bray's lips on my bite mark.

"Please, Bray, I need you, it hurts, I need you inside me, please," I can hear my whimper, but he just flips me to my knees, before I feel the blunt tip of his cock pressing into me.

"Open your eyes, kitten, watch your mates please each other while I fill your needy hole with my cock and cum."

My eyes spring open as Bray sinks into me. he pulls me up, so my back is to his chest.

Bram is lying on his back with Mateo on top of him, both with their mouths full of the other's cock. Bram's hand is partially shifting on Mateo's ass; the sight is pure porn, and it's all mine. My hand twitches wanting to stroke my cock to the view, but Bray spanks me.

"No, kitten, you watch and feel, I will let you know when you can cum."

I moan long and loud as he starts to rut into me. Bray might be a beta, but I love it when he gets all growly and dominant.

I watch Bram slip a finger in Mateo's ass. As an omega, I have a feminine build with slight soft curves, which I need for breeding.

Mateo was born to wear suits. he's tall and lean, broader than me, and he has muscle but not defined like my other mates.

Mateo and I could stand shoulder to shoulder, and Bram would still be wider than us. Seeing them like that makes me so fucking horny and the need to carry their babies is riding me hard, but I don't think all of us are ready for that yet.

I notice Bram's claws start to heat right before he sinks them into Mateo's hip, because of the size difference, some of his mark goes up his back, and the noise of them Cumming in each other's mouths is just too much,

"Please, Bray." I gasp, his hips still snapping against my ass, so hard I know I'm going to bruise. he pulls free of my ass, flipping me to my back before swallowing my cock, squeezing my balls with his hand. I cum in seconds, as soon as my cock finishes pulsing, he is pounding into my ass again, this time face to face,

"I love you, my Kitten," he moans out as he fills me with his release. he moves me closer to the others, and the four of us fall back asleep.

BRAMLEY

"Bram, I need you, my Dragon", Miles whines, pulling me from my doze.

"You never need to beg, kitty," I peck his lips with a kiss.

"How do you want me? Down your throat? In your ass? Mateo in your ass while I sink into his? or do you want me and Bray in your ass while Mateo fucks your mouth?"

Before I have a chance to say another his pained whimper lets me know he wants that, I pull him into my lap with my back propped on pillows, Bray lifts him so I can slide my cock into his ass before he starts to tease Miles's hole with his fingers.

Mateo appears next to me, and I pull him into a kiss. I need more than his cock in my mouth and mine in his, but later, when Miles is past his heat,

"Goddess kitty, you feel amazing," I husk before kissing Mateo again, stroking his cock so it gets nice and hard for our omega.

"You like watching them, don't you, kitten? You're dripping cum all over your dragon's abs, and your slick is gushing out over his balls and my fingers."

Mateo rips his mouth from mine before lapping at Miles's slick and my balls. His tongue slipping past his hole and joining my cock, Bray slips two fingers in with my cock,

"That's it, Matty, get out omega panting for us." Another two fingers are slipping in with my cock as Matt switches to the front, lapping the cum from my abs and sucking our whimpering omega's cock before taking my mouth again, making me groan at the taste.

Miles is mumbling nonsense as Brayden starts to ease his cock past the tight ring of muscle,

"So full, need more," Miles gasps out as Matt holds his cock like a prize before him. Miles opens his mouth and sticks his tongue out, "Greedy Kitten, Matty fuck his mouth while we fill his needy hole," Bray commands even though it sounds strained I don't think any of us will last, I hold Miles's hips up a little, Bray and I start to pound into him, after he's swallowed down Mateos cum his head tips back against Bray's shoulder, his hands sinking into Mateo's hair as he returns the favour and starts to suck Miles cock down his throat, Miles soon moans out Matts name, closely followed by Bray pulsing alongside me filling Miles with his cum.

When Bray pulls free, I shift and heat my claws, then sink them into Miles's perfect ass because of his size. My thumb is over his pubic bone, I growl out my release as Miles lets out a scream, covering my abs in his cum.

My beautiful mate passes out from his orgasm. We quickly clean him up and tuck him into bed before cleaning ourselves. Ember recommended just using water, no soap, as it might upset Miles if we fully wash the scents away.

Bray and I quickly eat something before climbing into bed with Miles and Matt.

MILES

I'm what Ember calls deliciously sore.

"You hungry *my heart* if you sit up, I will feed you." Mateo's lips brush mine; he tastes of pastries and jam. I pull myself into a seated position and flip a blanket over my still hard cock with a blush.

My cock isn't very big even when hard. I was embarrassed about it when I was younger, but now, I'm a greedy omega and like to be filled and stroked. I don't need to be big and fat for that.

Bray sits down to my right, passing me an iced coffee, which I sip at while Mateo hand feeds me a warm croissant with homemade strawberry jam.

I suck on his fingers each time, savouring the taste. No one talks while I eat, and I notice they are just watching me, so they must have eaten before they woke me.

I notice Bram is missing, but I can hear noise in the bathroom, where he eventually appears from.

"Come on, kitty, I've run you a bath." he picks me up and carries me to my big bathtub. he steps in and settles me between his legs, taking time to make sure I'm clean, and I pout when he keeps avoiding my cock.

"Behave, kitty, and relax," he murmurs against my ear.+9 I think I drop off and wake to Bram washing my hair, including using my favourite conditioner, he sits stroking my chest, his breath puffing against my ear,

"Bram," I pant and thankfully, this time his hand strokes down to where I need him, his big hand starts to stroke my cock, he only needs two thick fingers and his thumb, like I've mentioned, I'm not very big and my hips thrust to join him,

"That's it, kitty, chase it, take what you need, my perfect kitty mate," I cum shooting ropes across the water, it clings to the bubbles, Bram strokes my chest, whispering praise in my ear until my breathing settles again.

BRAMLEY

I step out of the bath with Miles in my arms. When he's steady on his feet, I turn to grab a towel, but when I turn back to him, he's on his knees and swallowing my cock.

"Fuck Miles," I bellow as my crown reaches his throat, and he swallows around me. I hear Bray chuckle, but he doesn't help me,

"Kitty, you need to stop, you need rest," he pulls me from his mouth, eyes brimming with tears, and his mouth in a full pout,

"Do I not do a good job? I need you, Bram, I need your taste on my tongue, my ass full of cock and dripping with my mates cum! It hurts so much. Why do you not want me, my Dragon?" Miles's voice is a pained whine. I lift him, kissing him softly. Matt is already on all fours, placing Miles behind him. I lie down, taking Matt's cock in my mouth,

"Time to multitask, Kitten. Bram is going to suck Matty's cock, while you fuck Matty's ass," Brayden runs Miles's tip over Matt's ass, pushing the tip inside.

"He's never taken anyone before, and your cute cock is a good start before he takes Bram's monster." Matt is speaking in rapid Spanish,

"I'm going to be rutting into your dripping hole while you scream around Bram's pet that he claims is his cock." I hear Miles's whine.

"Are you going to be a good kitten for your Mates?" Matt's fingers are gripping my hair.

"Yes, yes, please need all of you" Miles is panting, eyes on where he is inside Matt.

"Little pushes kitten, sink this pretty cock into your mate's waiting ass." Matt lets out a low moan as he is filled with Miles's cock, Miles is the smallest in all ways of us four, but being a Feline shifter, he has barbs that add to the pleasure.

"That's it, kitten, take all of me, such a good boy," Bray's voice is taking on a growl again,

"Yes, *My Heart*, fill me with that pretty cock, fuck yes, you feel so good." Matt starts pushing back against Miles, and I notice Miles stops thrusting and lets Bray set the pace.

I hear Bray say something, but not what right before. I feel a hot mouth over my cock 'Well fuck this feels fuck' The room is full of moans, curses in Russian and Spanish, sounds of slurping from me and Miles and the slap of flesh.

"Good boy, perfect kitten, are you ready to cum for your mates?" as Miles hums around my length, I cum, yelling out around Matt's length before he fills my mouth, I hear Matt and Bray yell out, but then I fall asleep.

BRAYDEN

Miles is curled up on my lap, eating the fruit Ember had sent up, "I think when Ren sets up his pack, I want our own place, even if it's a cabin near the main house like Grumps' place, but more us," I state to no one in particular, brushing my lips on Miles's mark.

"Mmm, Ember mentioned only having her and her mates in the main house, then others having their own places on the lands. Rens always said he doesn't want a traditional pack, so it would work." Bram chirps in between mouthfuls of his wrap (2 pancakes wrapped around fruit and syrup).

"She told me I would have an office in the main house, but we would have our own place; she doesn't wanna risk overhearing her brother having sex again or being heard herself," Matty says before feeding Miles some cake.

Miles chews and then drops a bomb, but doesn't seem to grasp that it's a bomb.

"Ember already has a place; her foster dad left her loads of properties, but she doesn't get access until your eighteenth birthday. There's an old pack house her foster dad shut down a few centuries ago that's close by and has plenty of land. She plans to get Bas and Timber to start fixing it up so that when you lot finish school, we can move in, and she's already talked to Mickey G about taking on Bram's care so he can come too. It's that fallen tree place we go to and swim in the lake." Miles eats a little more, and we just stare at him until he starts to whimper again, needing to be filled by something that isn't food.

Bram and Matty start to clear up as I start to see to our mate's needs. I make a mental note to have words with my sister; she doesn't have to do everything by herself anymore, and she seems to be taking on the role to start looking after us all, without letting anyone know.

MILES

I wake feeling refreshed and grateful that my cock is soft. I sit and flap it around a little, silently chuckling at the movement, my barbs wiggling like Jello.

I climb out of bed and head straight to my shower, avoiding looking in the mirror, my cock is semi-hard by the time I step out feeling the raised scars from Bram and Bray's marks and seeing the garter tattoo Mateo's spell left on me it looks like opal crystals in the shape of an infinity symbol, Bram has similar around his right bicep, once I'm clean and dressed, the guys are up and going through similar motions.

"You okay, kitty?" I don't have time to answer him as he pulls me in for a sweet kiss, which soon turns heated. Still in Bram's arms, Mateo turns my head, kissing me deeply, and then they end up kissing too 'fuck so hot.'

Bray comes out of the bathroom kissing me too before holding out a hand, and we head down for breakfast.

As soon as we step into the room, the guys, including the so-called grown-ups, start clapping and cheering. I slink into a chair next to Ember.

"Shush, you, but tell me your secret for not hobbling." She just gives me a shit-eating grin, which has me rolling my eyes while grabbing more food and coffee. Creed speaks up,

"Don't think your guys will let you have her remedy." He smirks, and I give him a curious look,

"Incubi cum is healing for their mate," Em says, then raises her eyebrows as Bram and Bray growl at Creed, who just chuckles. Mateo leans into me,

"I may have an idea how I can help, leave it with me." He gives me a peck on the lips and then turns back to his breakfast.

"Sis Miles told us you have plans for Rens pack house, want to share?" Bray gives Ember a what the fuck look, but she doesn't bait.

"Nope, I don't see how that's your business, Beta! Miles was told. As he will be overseeing the interior decoration."

Ember doesn't even look at him, but I would put money on her feeling Ren's eyes on her, who also seems to be unaware of this news.

"Sorry, Sweets, I didn't know you hadn't told anyone," I mumble, feeling like shit.

"It's okay, pretty kitty, I just hadn't found time," she kisses my cheek,

"And in the state, I imagine you all were then. I have a feeling if you knew them, you would have shared state secrets," She then heads off to get her work done for the day.

EPILOGUE

Miles

I know I'm pregnant. But the guys haven't noticed yet, of course, Ember has, and she is helping me keep my secrets. I also know I am carrying a baby for each of my mates, and I plan to keep that secret until they are born. I am just going to have to be sneaky about having blood supplements to help Bramley's baby, and Alma has given me some jewellery that will help Matteos. Now to think of names that will match. I wonder if Brayden will spank me for being a naughty, secretive omega?

But right now, I need to get our new packhouse and lands up to my standard. I love shopping for furniture.

THE TRIPLEMOON FAMILY TREE

NIKOLI IVANOVA — BUNICA IVANOVA

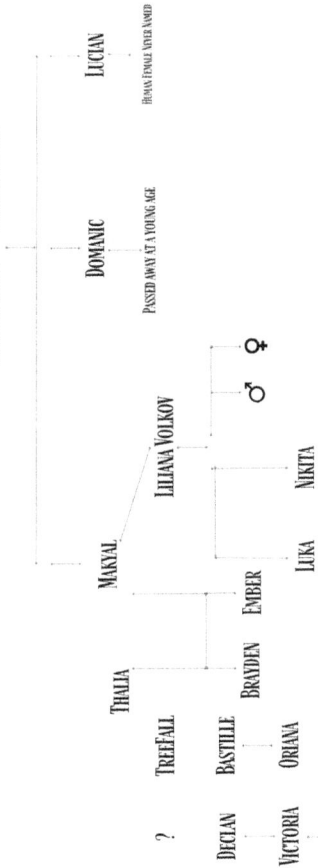

DOMANIC
Passed away at a young age

LUCIAN
Human female never named

MAKYAL — LILIANA VOLKOV

♂ ♂

NIKITA

LUKA

EMBER

BRAYDEN

BASTILLE

ORIANA

TREEFALL

THALIA

?

DECLAN

VICTORIA

♀ ♀ ♂ ♀ ♀

MILES

BRAYDEN

LACEY

BRAMLEY

BRONWEN

MATTEO

REYNA

27

PACK MEETING HOUSE

TRIPLEMOON PACK

SCHOOL

LIAM'S ESTATE

PENNY'S

GROUNDS KEEPER

GYM

CINEMA

XAVIER

KIRA

BLOODMOON

DEANNA'S DIY

DEMETRI'S

AMBER

CAFE

FINEST JAMES

CAITLIN MAKERS

XANDER'S CLINIC

KODI SHOWROOM

SAW MILL

FIND OUT MORE
ABOUT MILES AND
HIS MATES' FUTURE IN
BOOK THREE OF THE
BLOODMOON TRILOGY

ACKNOWLEDGEMENT

Thank you again to my Alpha, Beta and ARC readers for all
your help getting the BloodMoon series out in the world,
I think I would of given up if not for your support.

Another Thank you as always to my Family as there has
been a few moments where I needed their help.

I hope everyone enjoyed the series and what
it to come in the future for me.

BOOKS IN THIS SERIES

The BloodMoon Series

When Embers Become Ashes

A Phoenix Will Rise

And The Wolves Will Howl At The Bloodmoon

Miles Omega

MMMM Novella That Takes Place During Chapter Eight Of A Phoenix Will Rise

The Bloodmoon Anthology

Contains The Main Three Books and The Novella Miles Omega

BOOKS BY THIS AUTHOR

Lineout

Contemporary Reverse Harem Rugby Standalone.

The Forbidden Obsession

Book One In The Velvet Mafia Novella Series.
M/F Contemporary Romance.

The Wedding

Book Two In The Velvet Mafia Novella Series.
M/F Contemporary Romance.

The First Kill

Book Three In The Velvet Mafia Novella Series.
M/F Contemporary Romance.

The Princess Of Hell's Fightclub

Paranormal Reverse Harem Standalone.

Printed in Dunstable, United Kingdom

70457974R00030